CONFLICT RESOLUTION: POSITIVE ACTIONS

Grades 4–5

by

Martha E. Kendall

Published by Instructional Fair
an imprint of
Frank Schaffer Publications®

Instructional Fair

Author: Martha E. Kendall
Editor: Cary Malaski
Interior Designer: Mark A. Topolski

Frank Schaffer Publications®

Instructional Fair is an imprint of Frank Schaffer Publications.

Send all inquiries to:
Frank Schaffer Publications
8720 Orion Place
Columbus, Ohio 43240-2111

Conflict Resolution: Positive Actions—grades 4–5

ISBN: 0-7424-2788-9

3 4 5 6 7 8 9 10 MAZ 10 09 08

CONFLICT RESOLUTION: POSITIVE ACTIONS

TABLE OF CONTENTS

Introduction 4

Responsibility 5

Talking about Responsibility 6
Let's Be Scientific. 7
I Want, I Want 8
Writing a Job Description 9
A Job Application 10
On the Job. 11
Readers' Theatre: What Went Wrong?. . . 12–17
Reflecting on Responsibility. 18

Honesty 19

Talking about Honesty. 20
A Story to Talk About 21
Kindness Doesn't Hurt 22
We Volunteer to Be Kind 23–25
A Survey of Right or Wrong 26
A Fish Story 27
Be a Buddy 28
Reflecting on Honesty 29

Friendship 30

Talking about Friendship 31
What Friends Do 32
Making Decisions 33–35
The Fashion Police 36–37
Holding a Grudge 38
Friendship Comparisons 39
Prepare a Skit. 40
Reflecting on Friendship 41

Accepting Differences 42

Talking about Accepting Differences 43
What People Have in Common 44
Does the Difference Matter? 45
Take Your Pick 46–49
One Thing I Like about You. 50
You Can't Tell by Looking 51
Dear Abby 52
Making the Most of a Difference 53
Who Am I? 54
Reflecting on Accepting Differences. 55

Dealing with Bullying. 56

Talking about Dealing with Bullying 57–58
A Secret Friend 59
My Secret Friend 60
A Friendly Portrait. 61
The Power of the Pen 62
What They Did Right 63–65
Ask Abby 66
Reflecting on Dealing with Bullies. 67

Handling Independence 68

Talking about Handling Independence. 69
A Day in the Life of Nathan. 70–71
Who Am I?. 72
The Proverbial Truth 73–74
Pros and Cons 75
Help Your Buddy Gain Self-Control. 76
No Need to Nag 77
An Apple a Day. 78
Reflecting on Handling Independence 79
Conflict Resolution Resources
    for Children and Adults. 80

Published by Instructional Fair. Copyright protected.

0-7424-2788-9 *Conflict Resolution: Positive Actions*

INTRODUCTION

Children in fourth and fifth grade face increasing demands both academically and socially. This book provides opportunities for students from diverse backgrounds to practice strategies that enhance their interpersonal skills in the classroom and in other parts of their lives.

Creating a positive classroom environment can be the first step in the process. In a student-centered classroom, children learn by doing. They learn from what you say, but they learn more from the experiences they have in the situations that you create. As they mature, they can be empowered by assuming more responsibility for themselves and their environment. For example, instead of presenting a list of class rules that you have made, ask the children, "How are we going to treat each other?" If they suggest things like "no hitting" or "no being mean," rephrase their ideas into general, positive behaviors, such as, "We want to act in ways that keep us safe." Make a poster listing the children's suggestions. Refer to it throughout the year, and encourage the children to make additions. Emphasize that these rules are THEIR priorities; the children have a say in determining what their classroom will be like, and each child contributes to the group's success. Of course, it is your classroom, too. You will set boundaries that allow both you and your students to function and grow in an environment that fosters love and learning.

Conflict resolution strategies are effective only if participants want them to work. To encourage children to "buy into" the strategies taught here, every unit emphasizes the benefit of peaceful problem solving. Each unit suggests that you tell students about an experience you have had with the conflicts being discussed. When you share your personal experiences, you help to create a climate of trust and openness. Everybody has feelings, and children learn from your example that the classroom is a safe place to talk about them. Each chapter highlights phrases you can use again and again to help children internalize the understanding that to express their feelings, words work better than violence.

4

Responsibility

Fourth and fifth graders generally feel proud of their new identity as "big kids." Living up to that status, however, is not always easy.

Although large variations in maturity exist at this age, it is not unusual for nine- and ten-year-old students to outwardly direct anger when their choices lead to negative consequences. Admitting mistakes is hard. Conflicts arise when students refuse to take responsibility for their actions and instead assign blame elsewhere.

To increase students' self-awareness, this unit encourages them to anticipate and accept consequences for their actions. It also coaches them on positive ways to handle disappointments. Depending on the maturity and attitudes of your students, you may choose to discuss many of the issues before asking students to write about them.

To build on children's sense of their own power, this unit describes the role of Conflict Manager and encourages children to give themselves that responsibility. Finally, it provides opportunities for writing as a medium for reflection about their personal experiences handling conflicts and learning from their mistakes.

Learning Objectives

Children will increase their ability to

✓ recognize that choices yield predictable consequences.

✓ accept responsibility for their mistakes.

✓ handle disappointments.

✓ serve as a Conflict Manager.

✓ write about and reflect upon their handling of conflicts.

0-7424-2788-9 *Conflict Resolution: Positive Actions*

Talking about Responsibility

Try to offer examples of your own experiences as you ask students to share theirs. It's easier for students to be truthful about their feelings if someone shows them it's safe to do so.

Ask the following questions:

1.   What does it mean to be a big kid?

2.   What is the difference between a big kid and a bully?

3.   What are the advantages of being a big kid?

4.   What does accepting responsibility mean?

5.   What are consequences?

Read this situation aloud, and then discuss the questions that follow.

Steven could not concentrate. He sat in class watching the clock. The science fair was going to begin in about twenty minutes, and he could hardly wait. Steven thought his project was the best, but he couldn't help feeling nervous.

He asked his teacher for a bathroom pass. After leaving the room, he walked down the hall as if he were headed for the bathroom, but instead he bolted toward the gym where the exhibits were set up. He cracked open the door and saw that no one had arrived yet. He decided to take one last look at the competition, and he let himself in.

Wow, there are some really good ones, he thought to himself as he roamed around. I better head back to class, or else my teacher will notice I've been gone too long.

He quickened his pace. I know people will get here soon, so I better hurry, he thought. He sped up, swinging his arms high and fast. Then to his horror, he felt his hand brush against something. It was Mark's project, a chemistry exhibit with lots of glass tubes and bottles. It crashed to the floor, breaking into a million little pieces.

"Oh, no! What am I going to do?" shrieked Steven.

1.   What choices has Steven made so far?

2.   What have been the consequences of those choices?

3.   What are some possible choices for him now? What would be the consequences of each?

4.   People learn from mistakes. What do you think Steven learned from his mistakes?

5.   Think of a mistake you have made. What did you learn from it?

0-7424-2788-9 *Conflict Resolution: Positive Actions*

Let's Be Scientific

A hypothesis is an idea about whether or not something is true. In experiments, scientists test whether a hypothesis is correct.

Read the following examples of hypotheses:

If I make good choices, most of the time the consequences will be good.

If I make bad choices, most of the time the consequences will be bad.

Directions: Let's test the above hypotheses.

1. Read about Tina in the story below.

2. Come up with good choices for Tina and predict their consequences.

3. Come up with bad choices for her and predict their consequences.

Be prepared to explain the choices and their consequences to the rest of the class.

When Tina was sitting at her desk working on math, she happened to look down and see a ten-dollar bill crumpled up on the floor. It was near Miguel's desk. Tina thought, Everybody else is busy working on their math papers. I think I'm the only one who has noticed the money.

What choices should Tina make?

0-7424-2788-9 *Conflict Resolution: Positive Actions*

Name_____   Date_____

I Want, I Want

It is normal to want things, such as winning first place, earning an A, being chosen for the team, making the winning goal, being given a new toy or game, or getting invited to a party. Getting what we want makes us happy.

But we can't always get what we want. Everybody faces disappointment sometime in life. That's just the way life is. When we do not get what we want, we may feel frustrated, wronged, or just plain angry.

Directions: What can you do when you are disappointed? How can you make bad feelings seem not quite so bad? Here are some good choices. Add your ideas to the list.

1. Take ten deep breaths before you say or do anything.

2. Think of something else to do.

3. Tell a friend how you feel about what happened.

4. _____

5. _____

Here are some bad choices. Add other bad ideas to the list.

1. Hit somebody.

2. Scream at the person who disappointed you.

3. Break something.

4. _____

5. _____

Published by Instructional Fair. Copyright protected.   0-7424-2788-9 *Conflict Resolution: Positive Actions*

Name_____   Date_____

Writing a Job Description

Before someone applies for a job, she reads the job description. Usually, the first part explains the responsibilities, or duties, of the job. The second part lists the skills a person needs to have to be successful in the job.

Imagine that you have been asked to join a committee that is writing a job description for your classroom's Conflict Manager. This is what they have written so far.

The Conflict Manager for our class will watch for arguments between students. When one occurs, the Manager will decide whether or not an adult needs to help. If the Manager thinks that the students can solve the problem themselves, the Manager will ask each student to explain the problem, without interruption. Then the Manager will ask each of the children to suggest how they think the problem can be solved. The Manager will help them choose a solution. The Manager will write a brief description of what happened and turn it in to the teacher.

Directions: The committee is starting a rough draft of the second part of the job description. It will list characteristics of an ideal Conflict Manager. The committee wants you to decide whether the ideas they have listed should be kept or deleted, and why. Make your marks and write your explanations below.

Conflict Managers should be—

Honest: The Manager needs to report the truth.   **Keep** ❏   **Delete** ❏

Why? _____

Fair: The Manager has to listen to both sides.   **Keep** ❏   **Delete** ❏

Why? _____

Big: Children pay more attention to a larger kid.   **Keep** ❏   **Delete** ❏

Why? _____

Loyal to best friends: Managers need to help   **Keep** ❏   **Delete** ❏
the people they like.
Why? _____

9

RESPONSIBILITY

A Job Application

Directions: As a class, create a list of six characteristics that a Conflict Manager should have. Write them on the lines.

_____

_____

_____

_____

_____

_____

Now apply for the position of Conflict Manager. For each of the characteristics listed above, write at least two sentences explaining why you think you have that characteristic or how you plan to develop it. The application has been started for you.

To whom It May Concern,

I think I would be a good Conflict Manager because I have or am developing the qualities listed above that are important for this job. For example, I am _____

_____

_____

_____

_____

_____

_____

_____

0-7424-2788-9 *Conflict Resolution: Positive Actions*

On the Job

When someone is new to a position, he often gets on-the-job training. That means he learns the specifics of the job after he has been hired. A Conflict Manager can also benefit from practicing his new role in preparation for doing the job.

Directions: In groups of three, take turns playing the roles of two students with a problem and the Conflict Manager who helps them resolve it. Each group will act out their roles in front of the class, who will then discuss the conflict and the way it was handled.

The Conflict Manager will—

1. Ask each person, "What is the problem?" (Allow each person to speak, without interruption.)

2. Ask each person, "How can this be solved?" (Allow each person to speak, without interruption.)

3. Ask each person, "Which solution can work the best?" (Allow each person to speak, without interruption.)

4. Help them decide on a solution and shake hands.

5. Write down a brief description of the conflict and how it was solved. If there's not enough time to write this during the role play, the Conflict Manager can simply summarize aloud what happened.

Select from these conflicts, or make one up on your own.

1. One student says the other ruined the project they were working on together.

2. Two students have spotted a calculator lying on the sidewalk, and they both want it.

3. Two students want to use the computer, but only one can use it at a time.

4. One student has broken the strap on the other student's backpack.

5. One student claims the other has taken her bicycle helmet without asking.

0-7424-2788-9 *Conflict Resolution: Positive Actions*

RESPONSIBILITY

Readers' Theatre: What Went Wrong?

To perform in Readers' Theatre, actors stand in front of the audience. They do not memorize their lines. Instead, they use the scripts provided. There are minimal props, so these plays can be done anytime. For students who do not have a speaking part, they can create quick props, such as objects in the play or pictures of the scenery.

Actors are expected to speak their lines with feeling. They follow along as the other actors say their lines so they will be ready to jump in when their turn comes.

To help the audience identify the characters, each actor should wear a name tag. The name tags for the following play, *What Went Wrong?*, are on the following page.

At the conclusion of the play, actors and the audience can discuss the lines, the characters, and the play's overall themes.

Roles:

Narrator

Ms. Rodriguez, the principal

Brian, a student

Mr. Dayton, the teacher

Rakeem, Conflict Manager

Vicente, a student

Kim, a student

Megan, a student

0-7424-2788-9 *Conflict Resolution: Positive Actions*

RESPONSIBILITY

What Went Wrong?

Mr. Dayton,
Teacher

Ms. Rodriguez,
Principal

Vincente,
Student

Brian,
Student

Megan,
Student

Kim,
Student

Narrator

Rakeem,
Conflict Manager

0-7424-2788-9 *Conflict Resolution: Positive Actions*

RESPONSIBILITY

What Went Wrong? (cont.)

Narrator: The play begins in Mr. Dayton's classroom. It's about 8:00 A.M. on a Monday morning.

Ms. Rodriguez: During today's announcements, I need everyone to pay special attention.

Brian: Yeah, right. Boring, boring, boring.

Mr. Dayton: *(annoyed)* Brian, listen up!

Ms. Rodriguez: At our annual Open House next Monday night, we won't have room to display all the art projects, so we are going to select only the very best ones. It will be a big honor to have your project chosen. Work hard, be creative, and we'll enjoy seeing what you can do!

Mr. Dayton: OK, you heard Ms. Rodriguez. In our class, we're going to do art projects in pairs. In a minute, I'll ask you to choose a partner. But first, as you know, every two weeks we appoint a new Conflict Manager. For the next two weeks, Rakeem will have the job.

Rakeem: Thanks, Mr. Dayton. I'll do my best.

Mr. Dayton: I'm sure you'll do fine. I'd like everyone to give Rakeem a round of applause to show our appreciation.

(everyone claps)

Mr. Dayton: Thank you. Now I'd like everyone to find a partner for the art projects.

Brian: *(in a bragging tone)* Vicente, you're ALMOST as good in art as I am. Want to be my partner?

Vicente: Sure. If we work together, we can make the winning project!

Kim: Megan, those boys act like they are the greatest!

Megan: That's what THEY think.

Kim: Let's show them what you and I can do.

Megan: Definitely.

Mr. Dayton: Now that you've chosen your partners, go head and start thinking about what you will do for your project. You can work on your projects every afternoon this week. The winners will be selected Monday morning.

Narrator: Brian and Vicente began a life-size drawing of themselves standing side by side. Kim and Megan started making a collage.

0-7424-2788-9 *Conflict Resolution: Positive Actions*

What Went Wrong? (cont.)

Brian: OK, Vicente, now we've got the outlines done. All that's left is coloring them in.

Vicente: The drawings are big—just as big as we are. I don't think we'll have enough time to color them in completely.

Brian: Just work faster!

Narrator: Finally, Friday afternoon came.

Brian: Vicente, I have to go to a friend's birthday party after school. Can you finish up?

Vicente: I don't think I can get it all done by myself.

Brian: Just work faster!

Narrator: Brian left for the party, and Vicente stayed after school to work on the project. The girls stayed late to work on theirs, too.

Megan: Wow, Kim, our collage looks beautiful! I like to stand back and look at it and touch it, too!

Kim: We'll be done after we spray it with the glossy finish.

Megan: I'll hold it while you spray.

Kim: OK, here goes.

Narrator: The girls finished their collage. On Saturday morning, Vicente called Brian.

Vicente: Brian, yesterday afternoon I tried to finish, but there was just too much left to do. Mr. Dayton let me bring it home over the weekend. Can you come over to my house to help finish it?

Brian: Sure.

Narrator: Brian went to Vicente's, but he wasn't pleased.

Brian: Vicente, what have you done to the painting? Our drawing looks terrible the way you painted it! We need to start over!

Vicente: There won't be time to do the whole thing again!

Brian: Sure there will.

Narrator: Brian tore up the first painting and started a new one. He traced their outlines again and then began to color them.

Brian: This looks much better. But I have to leave. My cousin invited me to play miniature golf.

Vicente: How can you leave? I can't do all this by myself!

0-7424-2788-9 *Conflict Resolution: Positive Actions*

RESPONSIBILITY

What Went Wrong? (cont.)

Brian: Sure you can. Just work faster.

Narrator: Brian left. Vicente spent the rest of the weekend trying as hard as he could to finish the painting. Before he knew it, it was Monday morning again, and Ms. Rodriguez was giving the daily announcements.

Ms. Rodriguez: Good morning, everyone. Today the judges will select the art projects to be displayed at the Open House tonight. Please have them ready to show the judges when they get to your classroom.

Narrator: When the judges came to Mr. Dayton's room, they chose the winning project—Megan and Kim's collage.

Brian: *(yelling angrily)* How could they win? Their project is boring and stupid! ANYBODY could do a collage! It doesn't deserve to win!

Megan: *(yelling back)* Our collage is NOT stupid. YOU are! We worked together to make something really good!

Rakeem: What's the problem here?

Brian: Their project should not have won. It looks stupid.

Kim: You're just being a bad loser.

Megan: Our collage won, fair and square.

Rakeem: How can this problem be solved?

Brian: That's easy. Our project can be named the winner.

Rakeem: What do you think, Vicente?

Vicente: *(speaking slowly, in a quiet voice)* Well, I'm not really sure it's OUR project, because I ended up having to do most of it myself. There wasn't enough time for me to do a good job alone.

Brian: Vicente, I thought you could do it.

Vicente: I thought we could do it together.

Narrator: The end.

0-7424-2788-9 *Conflict Resolution: Positive Actions*

Name_____   Date_____

 RESPONSIBILITY

Readers' Theatre Discussion: What Went Wrong?

After the play, the audience can talk about what they heard and saw. They can also ask the actors how they felt as they read the lines.

Directions: Write your answers to the questions below. Be prepared to discuss your answers with the class.

About the characters:

1. How does Brian behave? How does Vicente behave? _____

   _____

2. What are Kim and Megan like? _____

   _____

3. Does Rakeem do a good job as a Conflict Manager? _____

   _____

About the plot:

4. Do you think it could happen that someone would expect his partner to do more than his share of the work on a project? Has that happened to you, and how did you feel? _____

   _____

5. Did the girls work well together? How did the girls cooperate?_____

   _____

6. Realistic means something could really happen. Do you think the argument between the girls and Brian at the end could really happen? Have you ever heard someone complain about losing? _____

   _____

About the themes:

7. What does the play show about handling disappointment? _____

   _____

8. What mistakes did the children make? Do you think they will learn from their mistakes? _____

   _____

17

0-7424-2788-9 *Conflict Resolution: Positive Actions*

Name_____   Date_____

RESPONSIBILITY ■■■■■■■■■■■■■

Reflecting on Responsibility

Directions: Think about each of the following topics. Select one that interests you the most and circle it. Then write two paragraphs about it below.

1. Describe a choice you made and its consequences. What did you learn from the experience?

2. Sometimes the hardest disappointments are those we cause ourselves. Admitting that you have made a mistake takes courage and maturity. Write about a mistake you have made and how you handled it. What did you learn from the experience?

3. Write about your experience as a Conflict Manager, or why you would like to be a Conflict Manager.

4. Describe the biggest responsibility you have and how you are handling it.

5. Write about a conflict you are now facing and how you would like to resolve it.

_____

_____

_____

_____

_____

_____

_____

_____

_____

_____

_____

_____

_____

_____

_____

_____

0-7424-2788-9 *Conflict Resolution: Positive Actions*

Honesty

Most fourth and fifth graders understand the difference between the truth and a lie. However, as peer pressure becomes more intense as kids get older, students may feel that being honest seems less important than maintaining their social status, even if it takes a lie to do so.

To help students realize that honesty is always the best choice, we need to create a classroom environment that rewards truth. Students need to receive positive reinforcement to help build their self-confidence, especially when they might feel that lying, copying, or stealing could work better or be easier than admitting a difficult truth. Internal conflicts ("Should I or shouldn't I?") can be as challenging as interpersonal strife.

This unit reinforces the benefits of being truthful preventing conflicts, and dealing with problems when they occur.

Learning Objectives

Children will enhance their

✓ tactfulness.

✓ ability to tell the truth.

✓ skills in self-management.

✓ understanding that honesty brings the best results.

✓ recognition that learning from doing their school-work is preferable to cheating to avoid their schoolwork.

✓ ability to reflect on and write about their personal experiences with honesty.

Use praise to show students that they can get your attention by behaving positively.

19

Talking about Honesty

Try to offer examples of your own experiences as you ask students to share theirs. It's easier for students to be truthful about their feelings if someone shows them it's safe to do so.

Ask the following questions:

1. What is the difference between a fib and a lie?

2. What usually happens to people who fib or lie?

3. Have you ever had anything stolen from you? If so, how did you feel?

4. What does cheating mean?

5. What can be the consequences of cheating?

6. Would you rather be friends with someone who tells the truth, or someone who cheats and lies? Why?

7. Would you feel proud if someone described you as honest? Why or why not?

Published by Instructional Fair. Copyright protected. *0-7424-2788-9 Conflict Resolution: Positive Actions*

HONESTY

A Story to Talk About

Directions: Read the story below. Then answer the questions that follow.

Just before the morning bell rang, Layla saw CeeCee walking toward the school door.

"How do you like my new hat?" asked Layla, smiling and showing it off.

"It looks like something my mother would wear," said CeeCee.

"But do you like it?" said Layla, still hoping CeeCee's comment wasn't a put-down.

"You want the truth?" asked Ceecee.

"Of course I do!" said Layla.

"I think it's ugly and it looks bad on you," she said.

Layla gave CeeCee her meanest look and walked away, not sure if she was going to cry or turn around and yell something mean to CeeCee.

That's when she saw her buddy, Tyrone, her older brother's friend.

"Hey, Ty," she said. "How do you like my hat?"

"I don't think it would look anywhere near as good on me as it does on you," he said with a twinkle in his eye, "but then my head is so perfect, I'd hate to hide any of it." Layla laughed.

"What's up?" said Tyrone.

"CeeCee was mean to me," said Layla. "I told her I wanted the truth about my hat, but I think she just wanted to hurt my feelings," said Layla.

"I don't think the truth has to hurt," said Tyrone.

"What do you mean?" asked Layla. But the bell rang before he could answer.

I. What do you think Tyrone meant about the truth not having to hurt?

_____

2. Reread Tyrone's answer when Layla asked him if he liked her hat. Did Tyrone say he liked it? _____

3. Being tactful means telling the truth in a kind way. How was Tyrone tactful?

_____

4. Have you ever had your feelings hurt when somebody told you the truth in an unkind way? Give an example. _____

_____

21

HONESTY Always tell the truth!

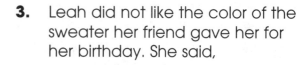

Kindness Doesn't Hurt

Directions: Put a check by the responses below that seem both honest and tactful. Many situations will have more than one good choice.

1. Tammy asks Anita, "Will you be my best friend?"

Anita answers,

____**a.** "No way, loser!"

____**b.** "I have lots of best friends, and you can be one of them."

____**c.** "We can be best friends for right now and find something fun to do."

____**d.** "I don't know. But whatever we are, let's race to the bus."

2. Shiloh said to the team manager, "I'm the best player, aren't I?"

The manager answered,

____**a.** "Everyone on the team has a day when they are the best."

____**b.** "You are definitely the best at being self-confident."

____**c.** "Everybody, including you, contributes something valuable to the team."

____**d.** "No. Antoine is much better than you."

3. Leah did not like the color of the sweater her friend gave her for her birthday. She said,

____**a.** "Where did you get this? Can I return it?"

____**b.** "Thank you for the present! It's a great style."

____**c.** "Why did you get me something so ugly?"

____**d.** "I wanted a new sweater! Thanks a lot!"

4. Sam asked Carlos, "How do you understand this? I don't get it."

Carlos answered,

____**a.** "I'm just smarter than you."

____**b.** "I'm good at math. You're good at other stuff."

____**c.** "You're stupid."

____**d.** "It just comes easy to me."

0-7424-2788-9 *Conflict Resolution: Positive Actions*

We Volunteer to Be Kind

Divide your students into groups of two. Cut apart the situations on pages 24 and 25. Place them in a basket or shoebox. Have each pair of students draw a slip from the basket or shoebox. Ask students to stop and think about how the students in the situation can be both kind and honest. Have them role-play their interaction in their small group using the words provided on the slip as well as ones that they make up. Their goal is to demonstrate how a kind, honest person can respond to a difficult question or comment.

When it's time to have students present their skits to the class, have a student from each pair read the prompt aloud so everyone knows the situation. Then each pair will present their role-play. Then other students can ask the actors questions and discuss what they have presented.

0-7424-2788-9 *Conflict Resolution: Positive Actions*

We Volunteer to Be Kind (cont.)

Use the situations on this page and the next page with the directions on page 23.

✂ -

1. One person says, "Here's a present for you."
The other person opens it and thinks, I don't especially like this shirt. What can I say that's both true and kind?

✂ -

2. One person says, "Do you like my new shoes?"
The other person thinks, They are not cool. What can I say that's both true and kind?

✂ -

3. One person says, "Why are you so much smarter in math than I am?"
The other person thinks, How can I answer kindly and truthfully?

✂ -

4. One person asks, "Why are some kids so mean to me?"
The other person thinks, How can I answer kindly and truthfully?

✂ -

5. One person who has a learning disability asks, "Why is school so hard for me and easy for you?" The other person thinks, How can I answer kindly and truthfully?

✂ -

6. One person says, "Why are you so good in sports compared to me?"
The other person thinks, What can I say that is kind and honest?

✂ -

7. One person says, "Everybody else's family has more money than mine. It makes me feel bad." The other person thinks, How can I respond kindly and truthfully?

✂ -

24

We Volunteer to Be Kind (cont.)

✂ --

8. One person asks, "How come you always get better grades than I do?"
    The other person thinks, How can I answer kindly and truthfully?

✂ --

9. One person asks, "Why do the other kids like you better than me?"
    The other person thinks, How can I answer kindly and truthfully?

✂ --

10. One person says, "I feel so dumb compared to you."
    The other person thinks, What can I say that is kind and true?

✂ --

11. One person asks, "What can I do to have lots of friends like you do?"
    The other person thinks, How can I answer kindly and truthfully?

✂ --

12. One person asks, "How can I be as popular as you?"
    The other person thinks, How can I answer kindly and truthfully?

✂ --

13. One person asks, "I just got a new haircut. Do you like it?"
    The other person thinks the haircut is not in style, but before saying
    anything, thinks, How can I answer kindly and truthfully?

✂ --

14. One person asks, "How do you like my new jacket?"
    The other person thinks the jacket is ugly, but before saying anything,
    thinks, How can I answer kindly and truthfully?

✂ --

15. One person asks, "I brought a cake I made to school today. Would you
    like a piece?" The other person thinks the cake looks awful, but before
    saying anything, thinks, How can I answer kindly and truthfully?

✂ --

Published by Instructional Fair. Copyright protected.   0-7424-2788-9 *Conflict Resolution: Positive Actions*

Name_____   Date_____

A Survey of Right or Wrong

Directions: Read each situation below. Put a check in the Honest or Dishonest column to show how you feel about the behavior of the people in the situation.

Examples	Honest	Dishonest
1. Shannon copied the answer to a math problem from Madison's paper.		
2. Erica said to Nasreen, "After school, let's go to the Tutoring Room to get help with our history reports."		
3. Chris got 100% on his homework because his older brother did it for him.		
4. Tara said, "Katie, I'll invite you to my party if you do my science homework for me."		
5. Jeff finished all but one of the problems in his math homework. He asked the classroom helper, "Will you help me with this one?"		
6. Sean offered this deal to Than: "I'll give you one of my CDs if you do my book report for me."		
7. LaKeesha suggested to her friend, "Let's look through the teacher's desk during lunch to find the answer key for the science test."		
8. Sarah asked her father, "Will you help me do my science project? Everybody else's parents are helping them do theirs."		
9. Gregorio said to Danny, "I'll help you with math if you'll help me with science."		
10. José thought, "If I want to get an A on my report card, I better start doing my homework."		

26

HONESTY

A Fish Story

Directions: A proverb is a saying that expresses a truth. Read the proverb below. Then answer the questions about it.

Give a man a fish, and he eats for a day.
Teach him to fish, and he eats for a lifetime.

I. Explain what this proverb means. _____

_____

2. When you go to school, are you being given a fish, or are you learning how to fish? Explain. _____

_____

3. If someone copies someone else's work, he is learning to steal instead of learning to fish. What kinds of difficulties do you think he will have in the future? _____

_____

4. Describe a specific example of your "learning how to fish" in school.

_____

_____

5. How will what you're learning in school help you in the future?

_____

_____

0-7424-2788-9 *Conflict Resolution: Positive Actions*

HONESTY

Always tell the truth!

Be a Buddy

In many schools, older students are "buddies" for younger students. They serve as role models who help the younger students understand what is important and how to succeed.

Directions: Imagine that you have received this letter from your second-grade "buddy." Write a reply that gives positive suggestions of how your buddy can solve her conflict.

Dear Buddy,

    I have trouble with my school work. My older sister says if I give her my allowance, she will do my work for me.

    What should I do and why?

                Thanks,

                Your Buddy

Dear Buddy,

_____

_____

_____

_____

_____

_____

_____

_____

_____

_____

28

Name_____ Date_____

Reflecting on Honesty

Directions: Think about each of the following topics. Select one that interests you the most and circle it. Then write at least two paragraphs about it.

1. Describe a time when it was hard to tell the truth. What did you do? What happened? What did you learn?

2. Write about a time when you lied about something. What happened as a result? What did you learn from the experience?

3. Write about a time you used tact to deal with a difficult situation. What happened, and how did you feel?

4. Are you an honest person? Write about yourself, giving many examples of how you are honest or could be more honest.

5. Do you want your friend(s) to be honest with you? Explain why and give examples of how they can be honest with you.

_____

_____

_____

_____

_____

_____

_____

_____

_____

_____

_____

_____

_____

_____

_____

_____

_____

0-7424-2788-9 *Conflict Resolution: Positive Actions*

Friendship

As students mature, friendships become more important and also more complicated. Many students in the upper elementary grades face daily conflicts involving power struggles with peers. They may feel pressured to appear to be "popular," to join or avoid certain cliques, or even worse, they may fear not being accepted at all. Some children have the misconception that the best way to look good is to make others look bad. They need to learn positive ways to solve conflicts and build their self-esteem.

Children who suffer from too much social stress may not be able to focus on academics. Resolving friendship issues positively produces not only a happier student, but almost always a more successful student as well.

This unit helps children recognize what true friendship entails and how to participate in a friendship.

Learning Objectives

Children will enhance their understanding of

✓ what to expect from a friend.

✓ how to be a true friend.

✓ strategies for avoiding or dealing with negative social interactions.

✓ how to deal with conflicts positively.

0-7424-2788-9 *Conflict Resolution: Positive Actions*

Talking about Friendship

Try to offer examples of your own experiences as you ask students to share theirs. It's easier for students to be truthful about their feelings if someone shows them it's safe to do so.

Ask the following questions:

1. What does it mean to be a friend?

2. What can you expect of a friend?

3. What does a friend NOT do?

4. Have you ever had anybody try to bribe you to be a friend ("Ill be your friend if...")? How did you feel?

5. What is a clique?

6. What does it mean to brag?

7. What's a put-down?

8. How does it feel to be put down?

9. How do you feel about people who put others down?

10. How can you be well-liked without putting anyone down?

You can trust a friend.

     0-7424-2788-9 *Conflict Resolution: Positive Actions*

Name_____   Date_____

What Friends Do

Directions: Read each situation about friendship. Then answer the question after each one. Friendship proverb: "Treat other people the way you would like to be treated."

1. Kailey and Julian were having fun decorating the classroom bulletin board for Parents' Night. Evelyn really wanted to decorate it, too.

   She said, "Can I help you?"

   If Kailey and Julian act like friends to Evelyn, how will they respond? _____

   _____

2. Ryan watched Jordan point at the A on her paper and say to Maria, who had a B, "I'm smarter than you are!"

   Maria's eyes filled with tears. Ryan wanted to be a friend. What should he say?

   _____

3. Antonio and Joe were hurrying toward the lunch tables. By accident, they bumped into each other, and Antonio's lunch box sprang open. The food inside spilled out on the ground.

   If Joe is going to act like a friend, what will he say and do? _____

   _____

4. Every spring the school held a big talent contest. This year, Keisha won, and Marcus came in second place. Everybody crowded around Keisha to congratulate her.

   Mohammed noticed that Marcus stood all alone. Mohammed wanted to be a friend. What should he do? _____

   _____

0-7424-2788-9 *Conflict Resolution: Positive Actions*

Making Decisions

To do this activity:

1. Make copies of pages 34 and 35. You will need enough slips so each pair of students has one. Cut the story starters into separate slips and place them in a shoebox or basket.

2. Divide your students into pairs.

3. Have each pair of students pick a slip. Have them discuss the story on it, and then share their answers to the questions with the rest of the class. Students who talked about the same stories can compare their answers, and the rest of the class can add their ideas to the discussion, too.

OR

Make copies of the complete pages for each student. Have volunteers read each story starter aloud. As a whole group, discuss or write about the situations.

0-7424-2788-9 *Conflict Resolution: Positive Actions*

Making Decisions (cont.)

I. Angelique and Zoe had been best friends all year. Katy was shy, and she didn't have many friends.

One day Angelique and Zoe got into an argument. When Zoe was watching, Angelique took Katy aside and said to her, "I'll be your friend if you promise not to talk to Zoe."

What should Katy do? What words should she use? Why?

2. Alfredo, Ben, and Craig seem to do everything together. In fact, they are planning a gymnastics act for the talent show.

One afternoon Danny happened to be standing next to Craig in their gym class. Danny felt nervous, but he worked up the courage to say to Craig, "I have been taking gymnastics lessons every Saturday all year long. Can I be in the talent show with you and the other guys?"

What should Craig do? Why?

3. Ascha and Jim both loved math, and they both loved to win. The teacher clicked on her timer and said, "Who can solve the most problems correctly in one minute?"

The children started to work as fast as they could.

"Time's up," said the teacher. She looked at the papers, and she said that Ascha had won.

Jim said in an angry voice, "I'm STILL better than you are!"

What should Ascha do? Why?

0-7424-2788-9 *Conflict Resolution: Positive Actions*

Making Decisions (cont.)

- -

4. Padma is hearing-impaired. She can hear only about half of what the other children can.

A group of children saw Padma walking toward them. One of them said, "Let's have fun. As soon as Padma gets close, act like you're talking normally, but instead, just whisper!"

The children all giggled—except for Molly. She felt like she was the only one who didn't like the idea.

What should Molly do? Why? What do you think will happen?

- -

5. Kaitlyn is having a birthday party after school one day next week. Her parents said she could not invite the whole class. Kaitlyn gave invitations to ten children. She wrote on the invitations, "Please do not talk about this at school."

Ana was proud that she was invited, and she wanted the other students to know. She asked other students in the class, "Did you get invited? I did."

Kaitlyn found out that Ana was telling other students about the party.

What should Kaitlyn do? Why? What do you think will happen?

- -

6. The teacher told Marcy and Laura to pair up to work on the math problems today. Laura has a learning disability that makes it hard for her to read numbers without getting them mixed up.

Marcy can't believe how slowly they must do each problem together. She has to read the numbers to Laura over and over again. Marcy is feeling bored and frustrated.

What should Marcy do? Why?

- -

Published by Instructional Fair. Copyright protected.   0-7424-2788-9 *Conflict Resolution: Positive Actions*

FRIENDSHIP

The Fashion Police

Directions: Read the story. Answer the questions on the following page.

As usual, Addy, Bethany, and Crystal were sitting together at lunch. Crystal said, "Have you ever noticed that some girls in our class have no sense of style?"

Addy and Bethany nodded in agreement.

Crystal said, "I think we should form the Fashion Police to tell the girls who are not dressing well to WAKE UP!"

Addy and Bethany nodded in agreement.

"OK," said Crystal. "I'll make cards and write on them with big red letters, 'You have a problem. Learn how to dress in style! Signed, the Fashion Police.' What do you think?"

Addy and Bethany nodded in agreement.

The next day, Crystal brought the cards and handed them to Addy and Bethany. She said, "Go back into the classroom before lunch period ends, and leave these on the desks of Melissa, Alice, Mary Jo, and Monica. OK?"

Addy and Bethany nodded in agreement. They left the cafeteria and hurried back to the classroom.

Crystal was the last person to come into the classroom after lunch.

Melissa, Alice, Mary Jo, and Monica had found the cards on their desks. Their faces showed how hurt and upset they were. Ms. Johnson noticed.

"What's wrong?" she asked them.

"Oh, nothing," said Alice. She felt too embarrassed to explain.

"Somebody did something very mean," said Mary Jo.

"Can a Conflict Manager handle the problem?" asked Ms. Johnson.

"No," she said, "because we don't know who did it." She looked like she was about to cry.

Melissa looked down at her desk. She felt ashamed, and she hoped nobody would know she had also found a card on her desk.

Ms. Johnson asked the class, "Does anyone know anything about this?"

Addy and Bethany looked straight ahead, acting as if they had nothing to do with it. Crystal pretended to search for something inside her desk, but as she pulled a book out, some cards and a bright red marking pen fell to the floor. Alice saw them, and she raised her hand.

0-7424-2788-9 *Conflict Resolution: Positive Actions*

The Fashion Police (cont.)

Directions: Write your answers to the questions below. Be prepared to discuss your answers with the class. Refer to the story for support and details.

1. Who is the leader of the clique? _____

2. Do you think Crystal was trying to help some of the girls learn to dress more fashionably? _____

3. Why do you think Addy and Bethany went along with the plan?

   _____

   _____

4. Do you think Crystal, Addy, and Bethany should get into trouble? _____

   What should happen to them? _____

   _____

5. How would you feel if you were one of the girls who received a card?

   _____

   _____

6. Why do you think Crystal, Addy, and Bethany were mean to the other girls?

   _____

   _____

7. Would you want to be friends with Crystal, Addy, and Bethany? _____

   Why? _____

   _____

> You have a problem.
> Learn how to dress in style!
>
> – The Fashion Police

0-7424-2788-9 *Conflict Resolution: Positive Actions*

FRIENDSHIP

Holding a Grudge

To hold a grudge means to not forgive somebody for a mistake the person made. Maybe the person said or did something unkind. Maybe the person apologized, or maybe not. But if the person who was hurt does not let go of the hurt feelings, she holds a grudge and prolongs the pain.

Directions: Imagine you just received this note from your friend, Jasmine. Write a reply that suggests a positive way for her to get past her grudge.

I feel so angry. MacKenzie made fun of me yesterday in front of our friends. She called me last night to say she was sorry, but she can't get off that easy. Today she asked me to come to her house after school, but I pretended I didn't even hear her. This is no fun. How can I feel better?

Dear MacKenzie,

_____

_____

_____

_____

_____

_____

_____

_____

_____

_____

_____

0-7424-2788-9 *Conflict Resolution: Positive Actions*

Name_____   Date_____

Friendship Comparisons

When you think of a friend, is it someone who thinks he is better than other people? There are expressions that describe people who think they are better than others. For example, if a boy is "full of himself" or a girl has a "big head," it means they think too highly of themselves.

Or if somebody walks with her "nose in the air," it does not mean she is trying to smell something. She thinks she is better than the people around her. Do these sound like good people to have as friends? How would you describe a good friend?

Directions: Finish the sentence to create your own description of a good friend. Make a drawing to go with it. Be as creative as you wish!

A good friend is like a _____.

0-7424-2788-9 *Conflict Resolution: Positive Actions*

FRIENDSHIP

Prepare a Skit

In groups of three, select one of these skits and plan a way to act it out. Then, practice it together. When all the groups are ready, each will present a skit. Classmates will guess which scene each group has enacted.

Scene A—The Putdowns

Three students: One student puts the others down, one student has her feelings hurt, and the other says it's not OK to put other people down.

Scene B—The Gossips

Three students: Two students say mean things about a child who is not present, and the third explains to them why their behavior is not OK.

Scene C—Following the Crowd

Three students: Two are planning to do something naughty, and the third child refuses to go along with it.

Scene D—The Clique

Three students: Two students refuse to let the third join them until the third uses words to explain why they are not being kind.

Scene E—The Braggers

Three students: Two brag about themselves, and one is not impressed.

Scene F—The Grudge-Holder

Three students: Two students invite a third to join them in doing something fun, but the third refuses because the pair did something to make him feel bad the week before. The first two apologize and kindly ask him to forgive them, which he does.

40

0-7424-2788-9 Conflict Resolution: Positive Actions

 **FRIENDSHIP**

Reflecting on Friendship

Directions: Circle the topic below that interests you the most and write at least two paragraphs in response to the questions about it.

1. What can you expect from a friend? List at least two qualities of a good friend, and give an example of each.

2. How can you be a true friend? List at least two ways you can be a true friend, and give an example of each.

3. "The Golden Rule" says you should treat other people the way you would like to be treated. Describe a time when you behaved in a way that lived up to the Golden Rule.

4. What can you do if someone is not acting like a good friend? Describe a situation in which someone did not act like a good friend, and explain how you responded or how you wish you had responded.

5. Nobody is perfect. We all make mistakes, and we try to learn from them. Write about a time you made a mistake and did not act like a true friend. Explain what happened and what you learned.

_____

_____

_____

_____

_____

_____

_____

_____

_____

_____

_____

_____

0-7424-2788-9 *Conflict Resolution: Positive Actions*

Accepting Differences

At a time when fitting in grows more important, fourth and fifth graders must learn to accept children who may not speak, dress, look, or act like most of their peers. Although it is normal and healthy for children to form groups of friends, it is essential that students show respect and kindness toward all their classmates.

Learning Objectives

Children will begin to
✓ understand others' feelings.

✓ appreciate individual differences.

✓ tolerate deviant behavior caused by learning or emotional disorders.

✓ speak honestly and kindly about differences.

Most fourth and fifth graders have learned that it is not OK to make fun of people with physical disabilities. They are likely to have more difficulty, however, dealing with students who manifest deviant behavior caused by invisible factors, such as neurobiological or emotional disorders. With a family's permission, share information with your students to help them understand the behavior of students with such conditions.

Providing a secure classroom in which all students feel safe and respected enhances a sense of community. In an environment that expects and rewards interpersonal acceptance, students are more likely to feel self-confident and willing to expand their comfort zones.

This unit teaches ways to not only resolve conflicts but to prevent them as well. It begins life-long lessons in fostering a culture that accepts diversity.

0-7424-2788-9 *Conflict Resolution: Positive Actions*

Talking about Accepting Differences

Try to offer examples of your own experiences as you ask students to share theirs. It's easier for students to be truthful about their feelings if someone shows them it's safe to do so.

Ask the following questions:

1. If you hear somebody calling people names, what words can you use to try to stop it?

2. When is teasing OK?

3. How can you tell when teasing is not OK?

4. How can differences make our class more interesting and fun?

Read this story and then discuss the questions that follow.

Helen and LaSheema were putting on their costumes for the holiday play. Helen pointed her finger at LaSheema and laughed.

She said, "Your hair is so curly that the hat sits on your hair, not on your head!" She laughed some more, and called another girl over. "Look at Curly Head, Curly Head, Curly Head!" They laughed, but LaSheema looked like she was about to cry.

1. Who used words in a hurtful way?

2. How did LaSheema feel?

Read the same story but with a different ending. Discuss the questions.

Helen and LaSheema were putting on their costumes for the holiday play. Helen pointed her finger at LaSheema and laughed.

She said, "Your hair is so curly that the hat sits on your hair, not on your head!"

LaSheema said, "I don't like it when you make fun of my hair. That hurts my feelings."

Helen said, "I'm sorry. I didn't mean to hurt your feelings. I'll stop teasing you."

The girls smiled, and they both felt better.

1. What words did LaSheema use to stop Helen's teasing?

2. How did the girls feel after LaSheema spoke up?

0-7424-2788-9 *Conflict Resolution: Positive Actions*

Name_____   Date_____

What People Have in Common

Even though you may be very different from kids from another state or country, you still have things in common with them, such as…

Clothing	Families
School	Celebrations
Food	Language
Places to Live	Music

Directions: Pick a topic that interests you and write it in the middle circle in the Differences Web below. In the other circles, write examples of the topic you chose. These examples should show how different one topic can be from person to person or culture to culture. Use an encyclopedia or the Internet to learn about other cultures, if necessary.

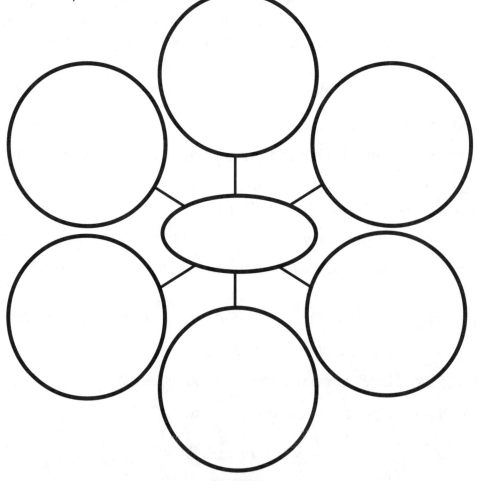

0-7424-2788-9 *Conflict Resolution: Positive Actions*

Name_____ Date_____

Does the Difference Matter?

Terenika is tall. Mai is short. Terenika can probably reach high places easier than Mai can. Mai can probably get into low places easier than Terenika can.

Sometimes being tall is an advantage and sometimes being short is an advantage. But overall, this difference does not make one girl better than the other. Most of the time, being tall or being short does not matter. In fact, most of the time, this difference does not make a difference!

Directions: Write three paragraphs about a trait that makes you different from a classmate. In the first paragraph, describe the difference between you and a classmate. In the second paragraph, give an example showing when this trait has helped you. In the third paragraph, give another example showing when this trait has helped your friend.

I'm Proud to Be Me and You're Proud to Be You!

_____
_____
_____
_____
_____
_____
_____
_____
_____
_____
_____
_____
_____
_____
_____
_____
_____

0-7424-2788-9 *Conflict Resolution: Positive Actions*

Take Your Pick

To do this activity:

1. Copy pages 46–49. Cut the questions into separate slips. You'll need one slip for every student.

2. Toss the slips into a shoebox or basket.

3. Ask each student to pull out a slip.

4. Give them a few minutes to think about the question on the slip they picked. Have each student read her slip aloud to the class and give her answer to the question.

----

1. Tanya plays volleyball. Melinda plays softball.
   Does this difference make one child better than the other? Why?

----

2. Bill likes to get up early. Nick likes to stay up late.
   Does this difference make one child better than the other? Why?

----

3. Juan has black hair. Kyle has blond hair.
   Does this difference make one child better than the other? Why?

----

4. Balinda has curly hair. Kim has straight hair.
   Does this difference make one child better than the other? Why?

----

5. Kirsten has blue eyes. Selina has brown eyes.
   Does this difference make one child better than the other? Why?

0-7424-2788-9 *Conflict Resolution: Positive Actions*

Take Your Pick (cont.)

✂ —

6. Michael has black skin. Austin has white skin.
Does this difference make one child better than the other? Why?

✂ —

7. Mernoosh wears a scarf over her hair. Margarita wears long braids.
Does this difference make one child better than the other? Why?

✂ —

8. Sammy wears braces on his teeth. Nate does not.
Does this difference make one child better than the other? Why?

✂ —

9. Juan speaks English and Spanish. Tuan speaks English and Vietnamese.
Does this difference make one child better than the other? Why?

✂ —

10. Patrick is a boy. Patricia is a girl.
Does this difference make one child better than the other? Why?

✂ —

11. Manpreet and his family speak English with an Indian accent.
Ping and his family speak English with a Chinese accent.
Does this difference make one child better than the other? Why?

✂ —

12. Cesar loves salsa music. Mary Beth loves country music.
Does this difference make one child better than the other? Why?

✂ —

13. Aaron does not come to school on Jewish holidays.
Li does not come to school on Buddhist holidays.
Does this difference make one child better than the other? Why?

✂ —

14. Drew's family is wealthy. Tara's family is low-income.
Does this difference make one child better than the other? Why?

✂ —

Published by Instructional Fair. Copyright protected.   0-7424-2788-9 *Conflict Resolution: Positive Actions*

Take Your Pick (cont.)

✂ ---

15. Marina lives with her mom. Madison lives with her mom and dad.
Does this difference make one child better than the other? Why?

✂ ---

16. Maria has pierced ears. Nicole's ears are not pierced.
Does this difference make one child better than the other? Why?

✂ ---

17. Adam is good at assembling puzzles. Elliot is good at drawing.
Does this difference make one child better than the other? Why?

✂ ---

18. Val's family has a big, new car. Luke's family has a small, old car.
Does this difference make one child better than the other? Why?

✂ ---

19. Matt learns most easily when he writes things down.
Mohammed learns most easily when he reads aloud.
Does this difference make one child better than the other? Why?

✂ ---

20. Jon has to work extra hard at spelling. Francie has to work extra hard in math.
Does this difference make one child better than the other? Why?

✂ ---

21. Dawn wears glasses. Keely does not wear glasses.
Does this difference make one child better than the other? Why?

✂ ---

22. Gretchen learns best when she has background music turned on.
Linda learns best when it's quiet.
Does this difference make one child better than the other? Why?

✂ ---

23. Sarah's family celebrates Hanukkah. Nayo's family celebrates Christmas.
Does this difference make one child better than the other? Why?

✂ ---

0-7424-2788-9 *Conflict Resolution: Positive Actions*

Take Your Pick (cont.)

✂ --

24. Adi's family immigrated to the United States from India.
Jesus's family immigrated to the United States from Mexico.
Does this difference make one child better than the other? Why?

✂ --

25. Allison was home-schooled for a year.
Evelyn went to private school for a year.
Does this difference make one child better than the other? Why?

✂ --

26. Lance is a fast runner. Brian is fast on the computer.
Does this difference make one child better than the other? Why?

✂ --

27. Kevin plays the violin. Connor plays the guitar.
Does this difference make one child better than the other? Why?

✂ --

28. Alex has a twin brother. Monica is an only child.
Does this difference make one child better than the other? Why?

✂ --

29. Angela's family speaks Spanish. Jessica's family speaks English.
Does this difference make one child better than the other? Why?

✂ --

30. Maya wears a skirt to school every day. Lisa wears jeans to school every day.
Does this difference make one child better than the other? Why?

✂ --

Published by Instructional Fair. Copyright protected. 0-7424-2788-9 *Conflict Resolution: Positive Actions*

ACCEPTING DIFFERENCES ■■■■■■■■■■■■

One Thing I Like about You

Directions: On the left, list your classmates' names. Write a complete sentence describing one of the things you like about each of them.

Name	Something I Like about You
1.	
2.	
3.	
4.	
5.	
6.	
7.	
8.	
9.	
10.	
11.	
12.	
13.	
14.	
15.	
16.	
17.	
18.	
19.	
20.	
21.	
22.	
23.	
24.	
25.	
26.	
27.	
28.	
29.	
30.	

0-7424-2788-9 *Conflict Resolution: Positive Actions*

ACCEPTING DIFFERENCES

You Can't Tell by Looking

Some differences are invisible, but you know they are there.

Directions: Read the description of Mathew below. Suggest a way to prevent a problem occurring before it develops.

Mathew was born with a behavior disorder. He looks like other kids, but he does not act like other kids. He tries really hard, but often he cannot make himself do many of the things that are easy for the other kids to do. He gets frustrated and angry.

Mathew especially loves to run. Everybody knows the rule that kids are not to run on the baseball fields when a game is being played. But everybody also knows that Mathew cannot remember rules very well.

When Mathew runs across the field, and other children are trying to play a game, what can they do to prevent a conflict?

_____

_____

_____

_____

_____

_____

_____

_____

_____

_____

_____

51

0-7424-2788-9 *Conflict Resolution: Positive Actions*

ACCEPTING DIFFERENCES

Dear Abby

"Dear Abby" was a popular newspaper column in which the writer answered readers' requests for advice about conflicts they were having.

Directions: Now it's your chance to write like Abby. For each conflict below, write your advice on how to solve it.

1. April writes, "I have trouble with spelling because I switch letters around. The other kids call me 'stupid.' They make me feel bad. What should I say to them?"

Dear April,

_____

_____

2. Beto writes, "I was born in Mexico, and my family speaks Spanish. I make lots of mistakes when I speak English, and some of the other kids laugh at me. What should I say to them?"

Dear Beto,

_____

_____

3. Carrie writes, "My mother makes me wear a skirt or dress to school every day. The other girls wear jeans, and they won't stop teasing me. What should I say to them?"

Dear Carrie,

_____

_____

4. Davey writes, "I was born with one leg shorter than the other. Some kids make fun of my limp. What should I say to them?"

Dear Davey,

_____

_____

52

Name_____   Date_____

Making the Most of a Difference

Many people are born with special abilities; however, only a few make the most of their potential. Great leaders in history stand out because of their special abilities. Maybe they were brave or smart, or good at convincing others to believe in his or her ideas. Famous athletes stand out because they are excellent at their sport. Creative people stand out for their ability to play music, paint pictures, write books, dance, sing, or make inventions. Write about  someone you know or someone famous who stands out because of a difference the person has that makes him or her special. Write the person's name as the title. Describe the person's difference and how he or she has made the most of it.

_____

_____

_____

_____

_____

_____

_____

_____

_____

_____

_____

_____

_____

_____

_____

_____

_____

_____

_____

53

Name_____   Date_____

Who Am I?

Directions: Select a famous person you admire from the list below, or choose someone else you admire. Write three clues that describe the person you have selected. Include the special ability the person has that has made him or her stand out. Begin with the hardest clue and end with the easiest. Use an encyclopedia or the Internet for help if needed.

Write your clues in the first person, beginning with "I." Present your clues to your classmates and let them guess the person "you" are. For example, if you chose George Washington, you might say: "I stood out for my ability to tell the truth, for leading an army during a revolution, and for being the first President of the United States.

Famous People

Susan B. Anthony	Amelia Earhart	Abraham Lincoln
Neil Armstrong	Thomas Edison	Rosa Parks
Cesar Chavez	Ben Franklin	Sallly Ride
Cleopatra	Bill Gates	J. K. Rowling
Hillary Clinton	Jane Goodall	Babe Ruth
Columbus	Martin Luther King Jr.	Sacajewea
Walt Disney	Lewis and Clark	Amy Tan

Write your three clues here. Remember to start each sentence with "I" and to save the easiest one for last.

1. _____

_____

2. _____

_____

3. _____

_____

(54)

Name_____   Date_____

Reflecting on Accepting Differences

Circle the topic below that interests you the most and write two or three paragraphs in response to the situation.

1. Sometimes it feels bad to think you are different from other people. Describe a time when you felt like you were different in a way that made you feel uncomfortable. How did you handle that feeling? Would you handle that feeling in the same way now?

2. Have you ever seen kids making fun of somebody? Describe a time you saw someone whose feelings were being hurt, and explain what you did. Would you do the same thing again?

3. Everybody makes mistakes. Describe a time when you did not act kindly to someone who seemed different from you. What did you learn from that experience?

4. What is good about having friends who are different from each other? Give examples of the benefits of your friends' differences.

5. Imagine that a younger student has told you that a child with a disability has joined her class. She says she does not know how to act toward the new child. Give her advice on how to act around this new student.

_____

_____

_____

_____

_____

_____

_____

_____

_____

_____

_____

_____

0-7424-2788-9 *Conflict Resolution: Positive Actions*

DEALING WITH BULLYING

Dealing with Bullying

It is normal to want love and power, but bullies try to get them in ways that hurt themselves as well as the people they pick on.

Like most of us, bullies try to feel good by gaining a sense of personal importance and freedom. However, their behavior does not, in the long run, help them achieve these goals. Bullies intimidate other people by hurting them physically, verbally, or mentally. Bullies use these tactics because they don't know how else to express their frustration, anger,and fear.

How can bullies learn to feel good about themselves without hurting others in the process? How can they find ways of behaving that will help them love and be loved, respect and be respected? Kind people gain respect and admiration of others by treating people well.

The activities in this chapter give bullies practice in engaging in constructive behaviors whose consequences feel good for all concerned.

This chapter also introduces ways for children to protect themselves from bullies. Empowered with these strategies, they own the basic right to feel safe.

Bullies and their victims both lose. Positive conflict resolution can teach them both how to win.

Learning Objectives

Children will enhance their

✓ understanding that bullies are weak, not strong.

✓ awareness of alternatives to bullying to get what they want.

✓ strategies for dealing with bullies.

✓ friendship-building skills.

✓ awareness of bystanders' power.

56

Published by Instructional Fair. Copyright protected.

0-7424-2788-9 *Conflict Resolution: Positive Actions*

Talking about Dealing with Bullying

Try to offer examples of your own experiences as you ask students to share theirs. It's easier for students to be truthful about their feelings if someone shows them it's safe to do so.

Ask the following questions:

I. Do you like bullies? Why?

2. Why do you think bullies act the way they do?

3. Have you ever watched a bully pick on someone? What happened?

4. Do you think bullies can change?

Directions: Read the following story aloud. Then have your students answer the questions on the next page.

Mr. Johnson announced to his class, "The School Board decided they want to speak directly with students. They invited one representative from each class to meet with them. At the end of the month, we'll vote to choose the student who will represent us."

"I want to represent us!" said Leticia.

"I WILL represent us!" said José.

For the rest of the month, Leticia was extra nice to her classmates. When Sara couldn't remember where she left her jacket, Leticia helped her find it. When Marie was sitting by herself at lunch one day, Leticia joined her. When David and Randy argued about who could use the computer next, Leticia suggested they toss a coin. They did. Randy won the toss. Leticia told David, "Let's organize a game of four-square." They did, and they played until the end of recess.

"This has been one of the best months ever!" thought Leticia.

José was also determined to win the election. He helped Juan and Vicente with their math. Then he told them, "If you don't vote for me, don't expect me to help you again." He told Ricky and Alicia, "If you vote for me, I'll choose

you for my team in P.E." At lunch, he noticed Laura had brought a big chocolate chip cookie. José grabbed the cookie and said, "If you vote for me, I won't take things from your lunch anymore." Laura hurried away, and José chuckled.

"I like being powerful," he thought to himself.

On the day of the election, Mr. Johnson handed out paper and said, "Please write down your choice for our class representative."

"Mr. Johnson," said José, "aren't we going to raise our hands to vote?"

"No," said Mr. Johnson. "This is secret ballot, so nobody knows who anybody voted for."

"That's not fair!" said José.

"That is a very fair way to vote," said Mr. Johnson. He told the class, "Fold your paper in half, and I'll collect them and tally up the results."

0-7424-2788-9 *Conflict Resolution: Positive Actions*

DEALING WITH BULLYING

Talking about Dealing with Bullying (cont.)

Directions: Answer the questions about the story.

1. In her effort to win the election, what strategies did Leticia use? _____

_____

2. What strategies did José use? _____

_____

3. If Leticia wins, do you think she'll continue to be nice to her classmates?

_____

_____

4. If José wins, do you think he'll follow through on his promises to his classmates?

_____

_____

5. Who do you think will win and why? _____

_____

6. Which behavior will earn someone more friends—being kind or being a bully?

_____

_____

Published by Instructional Fair. Copyright protected.   0-7424-2788-9 *Conflict Resolution: Positive Actions*

Name_____   Date_____

A Secret Friend

Directions: You and your classmates are all going to have a secret friend for a week. You will draw a name of one of your classmates and you will do nice things for this person for a week. At the end of the week, you can reveal your identity. Before you draw a name, however, brainstorm a list of nice things you can do for this person, such as drawing them a picture or eating lunch with them. Write your list below.

1. _____
   _____

2. _____
   _____

3. _____
   _____

4. _____
   _____

5. _____
   _____

6. _____
   _____

7. _____
   _____

8. _____
   _____

9. _____
   _____

10. _____
    _____

0-7424-2788-9 *Conflict Resolution: Positive Actions*

DEALING WITH BULLYING

My Secret Friend

Directions: Write about your secret friend.

Whose name did you pick? _____

Give at least three examples of nice things you did for your secret friend.

_____

_____

_____

Explain how you felt when you were being nice to your secret friend.

_____

_____

_____

List three people in class who were kind to you this week. Give at least one example of something nice that each person did for you.

1. _____

_____

_____

2. _____

_____

_____

3. _____

_____

_____

    0-7424-2788-9 *Conflict Resolution: Positive Actions*

A Friendly Portrait

Directions: Draw a picture of you and your secret friend. Give it to your secret friend when you reveal your identity to them.

Name_____ Date_____

The Power of the Pen

Directions: Imagine you got this note from a bully. Write a letter back with your advice.

To Whom It May Concern,

I spend most of my time alone. I don't like people because they don't like me. If I want something, I just push my weight around to get it.

I'm not very happy a lot of the time. What do you think I should do?

Thanks for your advice,

A Bully Who's Tired
of Being a Bully

Dear A Bully Who's Tired of Being a Bully,

_____

_____

_____

_____

_____

_____

_____

_____

_____

_____

_____

0-7424-2788-9 *Conflict Resolution: Positive Actions*

Name_____   Date_____

DEALING WITH BULLYING

What They Did Right

Directions: In the example below, the children succeeded in not being bullied. Write what you think they did well.

Patty waited in line for dessert, her favorite ice cream bars. Alex pushed in front of her. Patty saw Ms. Lopez standing not too far away, and she felt like going up to her and saying, "Alex is cutting."

But instead, she stopped and thought, "I won't be a tattletale."

Patty said, "Alex, it's not OK for you to cut in line."

Paula, standing in line behind her, said, "That's right, Alex."

Alex frowned and shrugged. Then he went to the back of the line to wait his turn. Patty and Paula shook hands and ate their desserts together.

What did Patty and Paula do right? _____

_____

_____

63

DEALING WITH BULLYING

What They Did Right (cont.)

Directions: In the example below, the children succeeded in not being bullied. Write what you think they did well.

Amanda had stayed back a year, and she was bigger than the other girls in class. When she wanted something, she said in a strong voice, "You're in my way." The children moved aside without saying anything. They did not like her.

Rachel told her friend Cari how she felt. Cari said, "I agree. Amanda is a bully. Let's tell her we don't like it when she acts big and bossy."

The next day, Rachel and Cari walked up to Amanda. Rachel said, "We don't like it when you boss us around."

Cari said, "You're not very nice to us."

Amanda was surprised. She said, "I thought you weren't being nice to me! Nobody ever talks to me."

Rachel and Cari were surprised. The girls looked at each other and burst out laughing. Soon they were all busy talking and enjoying themselves.

How do you think Amanda felt before Rachel and Cari talked to her?

_____

_____

What did Rachel and Cari do right? _____

_____

_____

_____

0-7424-2788-9 Conflict Resolution: Positive Actions

Name_____   Date_____

What They Did Right (cont.)

Directions: In the example below, the children succeeded in not being bullied. Write what you think they did well.

"I'm so much smarter than you," said Miles, making fun of Gavin. He always had trouble in science.

Gavin felt bad and looked down at his desk. There he saw his drawing, which Ms. Lee had told him was excellent.

Gavin said to Miles, "You are good in science. I'm good in art."

Miles was surprised Gavin had defended himself. He said, "Science is more important than art!"

Gavin said, "Science and art are both good. We are both good, too."

"Wow," said Miles. "I guess you're right."

What did Gavin do right? _____

_____

_____

_____

0-7424-2788-9 *Conflict Resolution: Positive Actions*

DEALING WITH BULLYING

Ask Abby

Everybody has conflicts or problems, and most of us can benefit from hearing others' advice on how to deal with them.

Directions: In the space below, write down a conflict you or someone you know is having with a bully. You can be truthful, but DO NOT USE REAL NAMES. You can also make up a situation. Describe the conflict briefly in the same way the writers did who asked Dear Abby for advice. Some papers will be read aloud for discussion and suggestions.

Dear Abby,

I am having trouble with a bully at my school. _____

_____

_____

_____

_____

_____

_____

_____

_____

_____

_____

_____

_____

_____

_____

_____

_____

_____

66

Name_____   Date_____

Reflecting on Dealing with Bullies

Circle the topic below that interests you the most and write two or three paragraphs in response to the situation.

1. Describe a time you were bullied or you saw someone being bullied. What happened, and how did you feel? Would you act the same way again?

2. Describe a time you protected yourself from a bully. Do you think you handled the situation in a positive way, or would you act differently now if you had it to do over?

3. Have you ever bullied someone else? Describe what happened and how you felt. Would you act differently now?

4. What are some positive ways to help someone who is being bullied? You can mention several, using specific situations in your examples.

5. What are good ways to protect yourself from a bully? Make general suggestions or describe a specific situation that happened to you or someone you know.

_____

_____

_____

_____

_____

_____

_____

_____

_____

_____

_____

_____

_____

_____

Published by Instructional Fair. Copyright protected.   0-7424-2788-9 *Conflict Resolution: Positive Actions*

Handling Independence

Will you make Kevin do his share?

Learning Objectives

Children will improve their ability to

✓ resist negative peer pressure.

✓ understand the various roles they play.

✓ control themselves when feeling frustrated.

✓ make rational decisions.

✓ organize their responsibilities.

As students refine their sense of themselves as unique individuals, they may experiment with various self-images that are likely to be subject to peer approval. Most fourth and fifth graders can distinguish right from wrong. However, they may need a great deal of positive reinforcement to learn that it's best to choose right, even when doing the wrong thing may seem easier or more likely to win praise from peers. Children are challenged to develop increasing independence at the same time that social pressures pull them toward group loyalty.

When children can solve intrapersonal and interpersonal conflicts based on what they know is right, rather than on what won't get them into trouble, they will have made a huge leap in maturity. To help them, we need to provide an environment in which children's good choices yield good consequences. A safe, trusting classroom is fundamental to that development.

This unit promotes children's awareness of the benefits that come from being true to an identity they feel proud of. It reinforces life-long lessons in courage, self-confidence, and self-sufficiency.

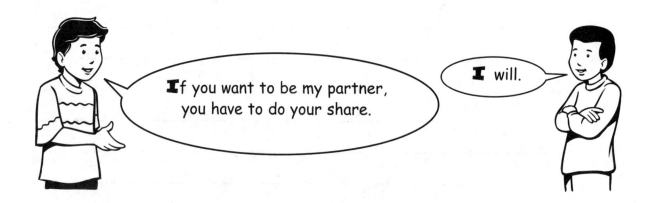

If you want to be my partner, you have to do your share.

I will.

0-7424-2788-9 *Conflict Resolution: Positive Actions*

Talking about Handling Independence

Try to offer examples of your own experiences as you ask students to share theirs. It's easier for students to be truthful about their feelings if someone shows them it's safe to do so.

Ask the following questions:

1. What are some good things about feeling like you're part of a group?

2. When can pressure from a group be negative?

3. What does it mean to think for yourself?

4. What does self-control mean, and when do you need it?

5. What does independence mean, and when do you need it?

Read the following story to your class and discuss the questions together.

At the beginning of recess, Landon joined a group of boys standing close together and talking by the classroom whiteboard.

One of them said, "Everyone take a marking pen, put it in your pocket, and follow me."

Landon asked, "What are you going to do?"

The other boys smirked at him. One said, "Be a guy. Join us. We're going to decorate the principal's car."

All the boys looked at Landon. He gulped and then said, "I'm not so sure that's a good idea."

"Are you a sissy?" asked one boy.

"No," said Landon. "I'm smart." And he turned and walked away.

1. Do you think the boys should write on the principal's car?

2. Have you ever had other children try to pressure you into doing something you did not feel good about?

3. Do you think it took courage for Landon to walk away from the group?

4. Do you think Landon should tell his teacher or the principal about what the boys are planning to do?

5. What do you think will happen if Landon does tell on them?

0-7424-2788-9 *Conflict Resolution: Positive Actions*

HANDLING INDEPENDENCE

A Day in the Life of Nathan

Directions: Read about Nathan's day below and on the next page. Answer the questions about each scene.

Scene One: Nathan at Home

When his alarm clock rang, Nathan woke up and went into his younger brother's room. "Time to get up, Benny," he said. Nathan pulled Benny's covers off and tickled him awake.

Then Nathan hurried to the kitchen where his mother served him toast and juice. As he ate his final bite, his father tapped his watch and said, "Time to go. Wear a jacket. It looks like rain."

Nathan put his jacket on and quickly slid his binder, baseball glove, and saxophone into his big blue backpack.

Understanding the scene:

Nathan has shown he plays many roles. One is an older brother. What other roles does he play in Scene One? How do you think he feels about his roles?

_____

_____

_____

_____

_____

Scene Two: On the Way to School

Nathan, Benny, and their dad walked to the bus stop. Raindrops started to fall, so the boys hurried to get on the bus.

"Bye, Dad. See you tonight," yelled Nathan as they pulled away.

At the next stop, one of Nathan's friends climbed on board. "Hey, Nathan," he called, "Let's toss the ball around in the gym before class."

Nathan frowned and said, "I can't. I'm supposed to walk Benny to his kindergarten."

"I can go alone," said Benny. "I won't tell Dad."

Understanding the scene:

What roles is Nathan playing on his way to school? How do you think he feels about his roles in this scene?

_____

_____

_____

_____

70

A Day in the Life of Nathan (cont.)

Scene Three: At School

When they got to school, Nathan grumbled, "I wish I didn't have to do this every morning." But he walked Benny to the kindergarten building anyway. To get back to his room, he took a short cut across the courtyard.

When he stepped from the courtyard into the hallway by his room, his shoes make a sloshy, squishy sound, and he left muddy tracks behind him. The custodian said behind him, "What a mess." Nathan pretended not to hear him.

His friends were playing ball in the gym. One yelled, "Nathan, come join us."

Nathan said, "That sounds like fun." But he shook his head and said, "Not enough time. Let's play at recess."

He hurried into his classroom and took his seat just as his teacher started calling attendance.

Understanding the scene:

What roles is Nathan playing at school? How do you think he feels about his roles in this scene?

_____

_____

_____

_____

_____

Based on clues in the story, list at least three other roles Nathan is likely to have as the day continues.

_____

_____

_____

_____

_____

Write about the conflicts you think Nathan probably feels about the different roles you listed.

_____

_____

_____

_____

_____

Published by Instructional Fair. Copyright protected.

0-7424-2788-9 *Conflict Resolution: Positive Actions*

HANDLING INDEPENDENCE

Who Am I?

Like Nathan, you probably play many roles throughout the day. Sometimes the roles might conflict, and you may find it hard to decide which role feels like the one that is right for you.

This diagram illustrates some of the many roles Nathan plays.

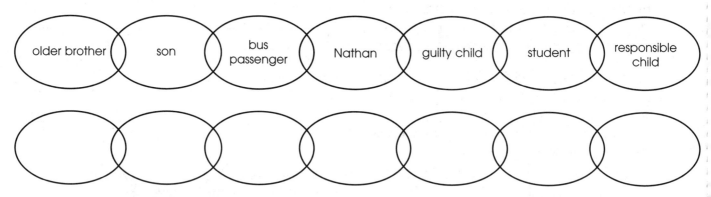

Directions: Write your name in the middle circle. In each of the overlapping circles, write down a role you play on a normal day. You may add more circles if needed.

Have you ever felt conflicted about your different roles? Give an example and write about how you felt.

_____
_____
_____
_____
_____
_____
_____
_____
_____
_____
_____

72

0-7424-2788-9 *Conflict Resolution: Positive Actions*

Name_____   Date_____

The Proverbial Truth

A proverb is a well-known saying. It uses an example to describe a general truth.

Directions: Working with a partner, discuss the meaning of this proverb and then answer the questions.

Birds of a feather flock together.

1. Draw a picture in the frame to illustrate this proverb.

2. What does this proverb mean as it relates to friendship?_____

   _____

   _____

3. Give an example of when children benefit from "flocking together."

   _____

   _____

4. Give an example of something negative that can happen when children "flock together." _____

   _____

0-7424-2788-9 *Conflict Resolution: Positive Actions*

HANDLING INDEPENDENCE

The Proverbial Truth (cont.)

A proverb is a well-known saying. It uses an example to describe a general truth.

Directions: Working with a partner, discuss the meaning of this proverb and then answer the questions about it.

One bad apple can spoil the whole barrel.

I. Draw a picture in the frame to illustrate this proverb.

2. What does this proverb mean as it relates to friendship? _____

_____

_____

3. Write an example about the effects of one bad apple. _____

_____

_____

74

0-7424-2788-9 *Conflict Resolution: Positive Actions*

Pros and Cons

Although some conflicts occur between people, others occur inside one person.

When one part of you says, "Yes, do it," but another part of you says, "No, don't do it!" how can you make up your mind?

Many people struggling to reach a decision make two lists—one with the reasons to decide "yes" (called **pros**), and the other shows reasons for deciding "no" (called **cons**). After considering both lists, they make a choice based on the consequences.

Directions: To practice thinking about pros and cons, imagine the following scenario.

You are the first person to come back to the classroom after lunch. You didn't like the lunch you brought, so you didn't eat much of it. You still feel hungry. A large box of donuts is sitting on the corner of your teacher's desk. They look and smell really good, but you are not sure what to do. Do you take one?

Make a list of reasons why it would feel good to take a donut (the pros).

Then make a list of reasons why the consequences of taking a donut could be bad (the cons).

Should I Take a Donut?

Pros	Cons

75

Name_____   Date_____

Help Your Buddy Gain Self-Control

Imagine that everyone in your class has been assigned a first- or second-grade buddy, a child you are expected to help.

You have met your buddy only once so far, and he seemed like a very wild, out-of-control boy. He can't take "no" for an answer, he doesn't think before doing or saying things, he has a temper, and he can never wait his turn.

Directions: Think of all the conflict-resolution techniques you have learned that could help him with his problems. Write about how you will use these techniques to help him. Be specific. Include back-up techniques if your first ones don't work.

_____

_____

_____

_____

_____

_____

_____

_____

_____

_____

_____

_____

_____

_____

_____

_____

_____

_____

_____

_____

_____

0-7424-2788-9 *Conflict Resolution: Positive Actions*

Name_____   Date_____

No Need to Nag

To be independent means to act on your own. People who need to be nagged to do things are not acting independently. They depend on others to remind them to finish their tasks.

As you have grown older, you probably make more decisions on your own than you used to. Many adults make lists to help them remember things.

Directions: List at least five things you need to take care of before you go to bed tonight. They can be things like school work or household chores. Be specific. For example, instead of writing "do my homework," name the assignments.

1. _____
2. _____
3. _____
4. _____
5. _____

List at least three things you plan to work on or complete in the next month. Think about big reports or long-term projects.

1. _____
2. _____
3. _____

List at least five of your goals for this year.

1. _____
2. _____
3. _____
4. _____
5. _____

0-7424-2788-9 *Conflict Resolution: Positive Actions*

An Apple a Day

"An apple a day keeps the doctor away." In other words, if you eat food that is good for you every day, such as fruit, you are more likely to stay healthy.

This proverb shows that doing something every day can help people accomplish worthwhile things. Shinichi Suzuki, a famous violin teacher, told his young students, "You only need to practice on the days you eat." He explained that practicing every day, even for only ten or fifteen minutes, would help them improve on their violin skills.

Directions: What projects do you work on day by day? Choose an activity you are proud of that you do every day. Write about it and how working on it every day has made you better at it.

_____

_____

_____

_____

_____

_____

_____

_____

_____

_____

_____

_____

_____

_____

_____

0-7424-2788-9 *Conflict Resolution: Positive Actions*

Reflecting on Handling Independence

Directions: Circle the topic below that interests you the most and write two or three paragraphs in response to the situation.

1. Do you have a particular group of friends you often choose to spend time with? Why do you suppose you get along with each other? What do you enjoy most about being with these friends?

2. Describe a time when you or someone you know felt pressured into doing something because of what other kids said. How did you feel? What happened?

3. Describe a time when you had to think for yourself. What happened, and how did you feel?

4. What does self-control mean? Describe a time when you had to use self-control. Did you succeed? If the situation happens again, would you act the same or differently now?

5. Name a conflict you are currently facing, and list the pros and cons for two different ways of handling it. Based on your lists, what will be your choice, and why?

_____

_____

_____

_____

_____

_____

_____

_____

_____

_____

_____

_____

0-7424-2788-9 *Conflict Resolution: Positive Actions*

CONFLICT RESOLUTION RESOURCES FOR CHILDREN

Bosch, Carl W. *Bully on the Bus.* Seattle: Parenting Press, 1988.

Kendall, Martha. *Conflict Resolution: High-Interest Stories that Encourage Critical Thinking, Creative Writing, and Dialogue.* Grand Rapids, MI: McGraw-Hill, 2001.

Romain, Trevor. *Bullies Are a Pain in the Brain.* Minneapolis: Free Spirit, 1997.

Romain, Trevor. *Cliques, Phonies, & Other Baloney.* Minneapolis: Free Spirit, 1998.

Webster-Doyle, Terrence. *Why Is Everybody Always Picking on Me?: A Guide to Handling Bullies.* Middlebury, VT: Weatherhill, 2000.

CONFLICT RESOLUTION RESOURCES FOR ADULTS

Ames, Louise Bates, and Carol Chase Haber. *Your Nine-Year-Old: Thoughtful and Mysterious.* New York: Dell, 1990.

Beane, Allan L. *The Bully-Free Classroom: Over 100 Tips and Strategies for Teachers K–8.* Minneapolis: Free Spirit Publishing, 1999.

Charney, Ruth Sidney. *Teaching Children to Care: Classroom Management for Ethical and Academic Growth, K–8.* Greenfield, MA: Northeast Foundation for Children, 2002.

Charney, Ruth Sidney. *Teaching Children to Care: Management in the Responsive Classroom.* Greenfield, MA: Northeast Foundation for Children, 2000.

Cohen, Jonathan (editor). *Educating Minds and Hearts: Social Emotional Learning and the Passage into Adolescence (The Series on Social Emotional Learning).* New York: Teachers College Press, 1999

Crary, Elizabeth. *Kids Can Cooperate: A Practical Guide to Teaching Problem Solving.* Seattle: Parenting Press, 1984.

Kendall, Martha. *Conflict Resolution: High-Interest Stories that Encourage Critical Thinking, Creative Writing, and Dialogue.* Grand Rapids, MI: McGraw-Hill, 2001.

Pasi, Raymond J., and Maurice Elias. *Higher Expectations: Promoting Social Emotional Learning and Academic Achievement in Your School (Social Emotional Learning, 3).* New York: Teachers College Press, 2001.

Sjostrom, Lisa, and Nan Stein. *Bullyproof.* New York: Educational Concepts, 1998.

Waugh, Lyndon D., M.D., with Letitia Sweitzer. *Tired of Yelling: Teaching Our Children to Resolve Conflict.* Marietta, GA: Longstreet, 1999.

Wiltens, Jim. *No More Nagging, Nit-picking, and Nudging: A Guide to Motivating, Inspiring, and Influencing Kids Aged 10–18.* Sunnyvale, CA: Deer Crossing Press, 1991.

0-7424-2788-9 *Conflict Resolution: Positive Actions*